Son Who Returns

Gary Robinson

7th Generation
Summertown, Tennessee

7th Generation, an imprint of
Book Publishing Company
PO Box 99, Summertown, TN 38483
888-260-8458
bookpubco.com
nativevoicesbooks.com

ISBN: 978-1-939053-04-6

19 18 17 16   2 3 4 5 6 7 8 9

Printed in the United States

Library of Congress Cataloging-in-Publication Data
Robinson, Gary.
  Son who returns / Gary Robinson.
    pages cm
    ISBN 978-1-939053-04-6 (pbk.) -- ISBN 978-1-939053-06-0 (e-book)
  [1. Indian dance--North America--Fiction. 2. Dance--Fiction. 3.
Powwows--Fiction. 4. Brothers--Fiction. 5. Chumash Indians--Fiction. 6.
Crow Indians--Fiction. 7. Racially-mixed people--Fiction. 8. Indians of
North America--California--Fiction. 9. California--Fiction.] I. Title.
  PZ7.R56577Son 2014
  [Fic]--dc23
                                2013043003

We chose to print this title on responsibly harvested paper stock certified
by The Forest Stewardship Council,®an independent auditor of responsible
forestry practices. For more information, visit http://us.fsc.org.

Contents

Acknowledgments

I want to acknowledge a few people for their assistance in developing this book. First, I want to thank my friend Pete Crowheart. He has danced the Men's Northern Traditional style for many years, and he provided valuable guidance regarding certain elements of the powwow parts of this story.

Nakia Zavalla, director of the Santa Ynez Chumash Culture Department and a powwow dancer, reviewed the manuscript and gave me advice on both the Chumash historical and cultural aspects of the story, along with insights into the world of the powwow.

Last but not least, Dolores Cross, a member of the Chumash Tribe and frequent consultant on Chumash issues, reviewed the manuscript and provided suggestions for improvement. Over the years, her efforts have brought important attention to the contributions of Maria Solares and her work with anthropologist J. P. Harrington.

My thanks to these generous people for their time and advice. *Kaqina'sh.* (That's "thanks" in the Samala Chumash language).

Son Who Returns

Gary Robinson

Chapter 1
Homesick

Life can be so unfair. Especially if you have no friends. And the people in your neighborhood look at you like you're an alien. And the kids at your school avoid you like the plague.

All my friends were in San Diego, California, but now I was living in Dallas, Texas. How did that happen, you ask? I'll tell you exactly how that happened.

I used to live in San Diego. In fact, I lived there for most of my fifteen years. Mom told me that she and Dad had met in college there. They got married and then had me. Or they had me and then got married. I'm not sure which came first.

However it happened, we were a happy family. That is, until Mom got sick with cancer and couldn't be cured. She died when I was ten years old. It all happened so fast. I honestly don't know why God allows awful things like this to happen to people.

Anyway, it's been five years, and I still miss her. I'm still not over losing her. I don't think I ever will be.

Dad seemed to get over it, though. Two years later, he got married to a woman he met through an Internet dating service. Her name was Eleanor. Dad called her Ellie. Whatever. I wasn't going to be calling her "Mom."

Things were bad enough without my mother. But after Dad got married again, my life started going downhill even faster. Dad's new wife, my stepmother, was so different from us. I've heard people say that opposites attract. Well, that must've been what happened here. She was white. We were brown. She was Protestant. We were Catholic. The list of differences was pretty long.

Don't get me wrong. My dad has always been a great dad. But ever since he remarried, things have gotten harder. First he lost his job. And then my stepmother threatened to leave him if he didn't get another job to support her.

They fought a lot. So, when Eleanor's cousin in Texas offered Dad a job, he jumped at it. Anything to keep Eleanor happy.

And that, in a nutshell, is how I got this way. Lonely, bored, and miserable in Texas.

I had to do something to keep from going crazy. A couple of times a week I talked to one of my San Diego friends online when I was supposed to be doing homework.

Dad had bought me a laptop computer for my fifteenth birthday in a lame attempt to cheer me up. It helped some, but not enough. Still, I was pretty grateful that some of my friends also had computers and we could instant message each other.

"Last weekend's storm brought in some killer waves," my friend Chuck messaged me. "We surfed Black's Beach. You should've been there."

"Don't rub it in," I replied.

"Here, let me show you the video clip we shot," he offered.

He played back the video, which showed up in the lower corner of the computer window. I could see my friends Chuck, Daniel, and Michael in their wet suits on their surfboards in the water.

"Who shot this?" I asked.

"Brandon," Chuck said. "He got a new waterproof video camera for Christmas. Now watch this part."

As the wave crested, Michael crouched low on his board, shot ahead of the other two surfers, hooked a sharp right, and zipped along parallel to the wave for a while.

"Sick!" I exclaimed. "Man, you guys have all the fun!"

Seeing that video clip made me miss California even more.

"I've got to figure out a way to get back out there," I said. "Are you taking good care of my board?"

"Dude, don't even question it," Chuck replied. "It's tip-top. Ready when you are."

"Thanks," I said. "Guess I'd better start doing my homework."

"Later, dude," Chuck said.

"Over and out," I replied.

I closed down the chat window and opened my online homework page. Let the fun begin.

But I couldn't really focus on homework. My mind kept wandering back to California. Back to my life as a young kid. I knew I had to have a serious talk with Dad.

The following night we had meatloaf, peas, and potatoes for the umpteenth time. Eleanor was big on the basics: meat, vegetable, starch, and iced tea. You had to have iced tea if you lived in Texas. I was about to barf on the basics.

After dinner I told Dad I needed to speak to him alone. So we went into his little home office. Sometimes he worked from our house, so he had a computer system set up in there. And he'd brought home other stuff he needed for his job.

"What is it, Mark?" Dad asked, after sitting down at his desk.

I took a deep breath and jumped in.

"You know I'm still miserable here, don't you?" I said. "You do know that?"

"Yeah, I know, buddy," he said sympathetically. "But I don't know what else to do about it. You don't really seem to be making much of an effort to fit in."

"You don't know the half of what I put up with at school," I complained. "For some reason these kids don't seem to think brown people should be in their class, and I'm four kinds of brown."

"I think you're exaggerating a little," Dad answered. "The people at my job don't seem to care that I'm a darker-skinned. Or that my parents were Mexican and Filipino."

"That's great," I said. "I'm happy for you. But the kids of the people you work with— the kids I go to school with—aren't like that. They act like it's still the 1950s around here."

"What do you want me to do about it?"

"Let me go back to California. Maybe I could live with one of my friends for a while. Their parents all like me."

"That's ridiculous," Dad said. "I don't care how much the parents like you. None of them would allow you to move in, even if I would."

"But—!"

"But nothing," Dad said firmly. "End of conversation."

He pushed away from his desk and headed out of the office. At the door, he turned back to me.

"You're just going to have to try a little harder to make friends and fit in," he advised. "You're stuck here unless you can come up with a better plan."

With that, he left the room. And he left me thinking. A better plan, he said. Okay, I thought to myself, I'll get right on it.

For the next two days I carried on a dialogue in my head. I'd come up with an idea for a plan to get back to California, and then I'd throw it out. Sometimes I was surprised at how lame my ideas could be.

But then, I was also surprised by my flashes of brilliance. An idea came to me that was nothing short of genius. At least in my mind.

Chapter 2
The Plan

My real mother was half Chumash Indian and half Crow Indian. That's what made me four kinds of brown: Mexican, Filipino, Chumash, and Crow. I don't know why anyone would say Indians are red; they never look like that to me.

Almost every summer of my young life I spent a month with my mother's mother, my Nana. She lived on the Chumash reservation in central California, near the small town of Santa Ynez. I only vaguely remember some of the things Mom told me about our Chumash culture and history.

The tiny reservation was smaller than most golf courses. I have to say it was beautiful there in that valley. A row of mountains ran along one side. Oak trees, vineyards, ranches, and orchards spread out for miles. And a river ran through it, stretching from the mountains to the ocean about twenty miles away.

And that ocean meant there were beaches. And where there were beaches, there was surfing.

I hadn't been back to see Nana in three or four years. A visit was long overdue. You get where I was going with this, right? I presented my brilliant idea to my father the following night.

"Dad, I need to spend some time with Nana," I said innocently. "What if I went out and stayed with her for a while this summer like I used to? I'm sure she'd appreciate a visit."

Dad thought about that idea for a minute.

"I bet you're pretty proud of yourself, aren't you?" Dad responded finally. "Is this the first part of your long-range plan?"

"What do you mean?" I asked with my best innocent face.

"You'll spend part of the summer with Nana," Dad explained. "Then at the end of the visit, you'll tell me you don't want to come back to Texas. You'll say you want to stay there and go to school."

"Wow, I hadn't thought of that," I replied. I hoped the surprised look on my face was convincing. "What a great idea!"

"You can drop the act," Dad said. "You forget that I was a teenager once myself."

I let out a big sigh. My cover had been blown.

"But, I'll think about it," he added.

That perked me right up.

"You will?"

"I'll even call your Nana to see what she thinks of the idea," Dad offered.

"Awesome!"

This was exciting news.

"I know things have been tough on you," Dad admitted. "I do want you to be happy."

He hugged me.

"Now go do your homework," he said, and I turned to go.

"And don't spend too much time chatting with your California friends online," he instructed.

"You know about that?"

"Of course I do," he said sternly. "I know everything," he added with a smile.

I logged in to instant messaging to see who was already online. Michael was there.

"If this works, maybe you guys can come up to Chumash," I told Michael online. "We can surf near Santa Barbara, or my grandma might let me come down for a visit."

"We'll figure something out," he replied with excitement. "I'll let the guys know you might be nearby this summer. Are you sure your grandmother will go for it?"

"Are you kidding? She loves to hang out with all of her grandkids. I lost track of how many of us there are. Twelve or thirteen, maybe. And a few great grandkids too."

Michael was amazed at the size of that part of my family. I really hadn't thought about it much, because all I'd ever known was my big family. I thought everyone had a family like mine.

After I signed off, I opened the calendar on my computer. It was now April, and school would be out the second week of June. I could stick around until after Father's Day and then head west. That should work.

I stopped myself right there. Nothing was worse than getting all excited about big plans that never saw the light of day. I didn't want to set myself up for a huge disappointment.

I put the calendar away and tried to focus on the here and now. Homework. That was what I was supposed to be doing. I concentrated on that with a great deal of difficulty.

I didn't want to seem too pushy with Dad, so I didn't try to get an answer from him for a couple of days. I tried to play it cool. I tried to make Dad think I didn't care about it that much.

When the weekend came, I helped around the yard doing chores. It was spring, and stuff was starting to grow. Dad was planting herbs and vegetables in his garden, like he does every year. I mowed the lawn and trimmed some bushes. I even dug up a few weeds. I was working hard. I think I overdid it.

"Whoa, whoa, whoa," Dad advised. "Slow down or you'll hurt yourself."

"Okay," I replied, as I threw a pile of weeds into the wheelbarrow.

I paused to take a breath. Then I let it out.

"When are you going to give me your answer about this summer?" I blurted. "I've been waiting for days!"

"Oh, that," Dad said in a joking way. "I'd almost forgotten all about it."

"Really?"

"No, not really," he answered. "I just wanted to see how long you could hold out before exploding." He laughed. "You lasted longer than I expected."

He continued to smile and not tell me his answer.

"Okay, enough is enough," I said, totally frustrated. "Out with it!"

"I'll tell you over a glass of iced tea," he said, putting his hand on my shoulder. We sat down on the front porch, where a tray holding a pitcher of tea and two glasses waited for us.

I guess Eleanor had put it there when I wasn't looking.

"I talked to Nana," Dad said as he poured tea in our glasses. "Of course, she's all excited about the possibility of you coming out for the summer."

"Great!" I said as I took my first gulp.

"And I talked to Eleanor about you staying out there to start high school," he said.

"Why?" I asked. I resented Dad talking to her about anything having to do with me. "She doesn't have any say over what I do. She's not my mother."

"Actually, she does have some say about what goes on in your life," Dad said. "She has ever since she and I got married."

"What? That's not right."

I was more than a little mad about this.

"Even though she's not your mother, she *is* a woman," Dad explained. "Men often need input from women to help them make decisions about their kids. Women see things differently."

I felt defeated. I hung my head. My stepmother had done nothing but ruin things for me up to this point. Why would that stop now? I waited for the bad news.

"She said I should let you do it," Dad continued. "I wasn't so sure myself. But she talked me into it."

I looked up at him. He was smiling.

"Are you kidding me right now, or are you serious?"

"I'm totally serious. You can spend part of the summer with Nana."

I jumped for joy. Literally. I leaped off the porch, and while I was in the air, I might have screamed, "Wahoo," or something ridiculous like that. I landed in the grass and rolled over on my back. The sky above me was a deep blue.

Dad walked over and looked down at me.

"And, depending on how things go," he continued, "you might be able to stay with her through high school."

I couldn't believe my ears. This was too good to be true. Just then, Eleanor stepped out on the porch.

"Did you tell him?" she asked my dad.

"Yep," he answered. "Mark flipped out, and here he lies."

I stood up and looked at Eleanor with fresh eyes. Maybe she *wasn't* the wicked witch sent to earth to ruin my life.

"Thanks," I said in a quiet voice.

"You're absolutely welcome," she said with a smile and a nod. Then she went back inside.

I immediately went back into planning mode. Actually, it was more like questioning mode. What would I take to California with me? What would I leave behind? When could I get my board from Chuck? When would I be able to get together with those guys? Did Nana have a spare room I could sleep in? So many details to think about.

That night I tried to find the guys via IM. I had to let them know it was a go. No one seemed to be around, though. So, Facebook was my next stop. "Its official," I posted. "I'll be back in the Cali sun this summer! Somebody tell my surfboard."

Within a few minutes, the guys had all commented.

"Sick," Chuck replied. "Let the hammer down, dude!"

"Dope," Michael's message said. "Peace on the beach."

"Epic," Daniel typed. "That's freakin' awesome!"

On Sunday, Dad said I needed to call Nana to thank her and to start reconnecting with her. After dinner I made the call. It was seven o'clock at night in Texas, so that meant it was five o'clock in California.

"I'm so glad you're coming out here," Nana said on the phone. "It's been too long since I've seen you."

"Are you sure you have room for me?" I asked. "I know it's pretty crowded at your house."

"We added two rooms to the back of the house since you were here last," she assured me. "You'll have your own room."

"Awesome!" I replied.

"You can get reacquainted with your relatives here. And meet some you didn't even know you had."

We talked a little while longer, and then I told Nana I had to do homework. On the phone I was all upbeat and positive. But I secretly had some worries about the whole deal.

Would I be just as bored there as I was here? Would I have access to the Internet so I could connect with my San Diego friends? And what else was there for a fifteen-year-old to do on the Chumash Reservation in the middle of the California backcountry?

Chapter 3
Westward Ho!

The closer the time came for me to escape from Texas, the less sure I was about the move. The worries I had grew bigger in my own mind. And the positive reasons for going ahead with my plan seemed to shrink. What had I gotten myself into?

Dad decided that I should stay with him at least until the fourth of July. By that time of year, it's so hot and humid in Dallas that you just don't want to go outside. It was better not to leave your air-conditioned house, unless you were headed for a swimming pool.

The day after the picnic and fireworks were over, I began packing for the trip. There was a lot of stuff I needed to take—too much for the luggage that would fly with me on the plane. So Dad boxed up some of my things and shipped them to Nana's house. They would show up a couple of days later by truck.

Departure day arrived. Eleanor stood at the doorway of our house and waved good-bye. Dad drove me to the airport and filled out special papers that were needed for a minor to fly alone on the plane.

"I'm getting myself a computer in the next couple of days," Dad said before I went through the security checkpoint. "Maybe you and I can communicate the same way you do with your friends."

"I'd like that," I said as I hugged him. "You'd better come out and see me, though." A tear formed in the corner of my eye, but I quickly wiped it away so no one else in the terminal would see.

"I will," Dad replied as we finished the hug. "Now you listen to your Nana, okay? You have to follow her rules."

I agreed, gave Dad one last hug, and then walked down the jetway toward the new phase of my life.

On the other end of the boring flight, Nana and my Aunt Dolores were waiting for me at the Santa Barbara airport. They both looked the same as I had remembered them. Nana had a long braid of gray hair and wore a long flowing dress. Aunt Dolores had short brown hair and a fringed leather purse with Native beadwork.

Of course, they carried on about how much I'd grown and what a handsome young man I was. They hugged me and patted me on the back. Typical grandma and auntie stuff.

We loaded my luggage in the back of Nana's red four-wheel-drive Jeep Wrangler and headed for the reservation. To get there, we had to drive up a winding mountain road and over what they called "the Pass," which was the only way to get to the other side of the mountain range.

Along the way Aunt Dolores pointed to a green sign on the side of that road that read "Chumash Highway."

"That's cool," I said, "having a highway named after the tribe."

"For thousands of years, the Chumash people traveled on foot back and forth over this same mountain pass," my aunt said. "Of course, it was just a trail in those days. The State of California decided to recognize that we were here first."

I watched the beautiful countryside go by as we drove. It hadn't changed since I'd seen it last. The mountains, oak trees, vineyards, ranches and orchards were still there. And the river. The river reminded me of the ocean and the beaches and the surfing.

"Take it all in, grandson," Nana said. "Part of you is from here. Part of you belongs in this place."

I thought about Nana's words for a fraction of a second. Then I launched into my tale of woe concerning my long lost surfing buddies and my lonely surfboard.

"So it would be really great if we could figure out a way to get me down to San Diego," I said as I came to the end of my story. "Or if there's a way for my friends to come up here for visit. As soon as possible."

Nana looked at Aunt Dolores for a minute. I think she might have winked at her.

"San Diego is a long way off," Nana said. "We never go down there, do we?"

"No, we never do," my aunt agreed. "I don't know how we'll ever get Mark together with his surfing buddies."

"We'll keep our eyes open," Nana finally said. "Maybe an opportunity to go to San Diego will present itself sometime soon."

None of it sounded too promising. I sat quietly in the backseat for a while.

After about half an hour, we came to a sign that pointed left and read "Chumash Reservation." Nana made that turn, which took us toward the little town of Santa Ynez. I remembered going into town with Nana when I was younger. The buildings all looked like they were built in the late 1800s or so; they were very Wild West–style.

And then we passed by a very large building that I didn't remember seeing before. Its parking lot was filled with cars.

"What's that?" I asked from the back seat.

"That's the tribe's casino and hotel," Aunt Dolores said. "That's right. It was just a small building the last time you were here. It has really grown."

We went down a little road that ran behind the casino complex and into the reservation neighborhood. Now we were on familiar-looking turf.

Nana's house was on what they called the "lower rez." This part of the reservation was located along a slow-moving creek. Other people lived up on a hill overlooking the creek in the part called the "upper rez." That's where the tribe's offices and health clinic were located.

We rounded a corner and arrived at Nana's house. I looked it over as I got out of the car. It was in better shape than I remembered.

"We had quite a bit of work done on the place," Nana said. "It needed a lot of repairs and a new coat of paint. After the casino expanded, we got enough money to fix it. We also added on the two extra rooms."

An elderly man came out of the house and walked toward us.

"This is my husband, Pablo," Nana said. "I was alone for many years after your grandpa died, but now I have Pablo."

As he got closer to us, Nana asked me, "Do you speak any Spanish?"

"I had Spanish in eighth grade, but I barely passed it," I answered.

Pablo reached the car. He put out his hand and shook mine.

"*Buenos dias, Marcos,*" he said. "*Como estás?*"

I think he said, "Good day, Mark. How are you?"

"Pablo doesn't speak much English," Nana explained.

I tried to remember enough of my Spanish lessons to answer him.

"*Muy bien, y tu?*" I said to Pablo. I think I said, "Very well, and you?"

Pablo's eyes lit up. He let loose with a string of Spanish words that came so fast I had no idea what he said. When everyone saw the surprised and panicked look on my face, they immediately knew I was in over my head. We all broke out laughing.

Nana said something to him in Spanish that I didn't understand. Then Pablo, grinning from ear to ear, shook my hand very hard, saying, "*Haku, haku!*"

Thankfully, I remembered what that meant. Pablo must have learned a little Chumash.

"That's 'hello' in the Chumash language," I said confidently.

"Good for you," Nana said.

"I guess that means you have to speak three languages around here," I observed.

"Pretty much," Aunt Dolores agreed. "Don't worry. You'll get used to it. Your Nana and I are just learning to speak a little Chumash ourselves. Weekly classes."

Grabbing my luggage from the back of the SUV, Pablo, Nana, and Dolores headed for the front door. I followed. Inside the house, I was surprised the find the living room full of people. A banner hung across the back wall that read "*Haku*, Mark!"

"Some of your extended family wanted to greet you when you arrived," Aunt Dolores said. "And here they are."

This gathering was pretty cool, even if it was a little overwhelming. I sort of felt like a celebrity surrounded by adoring fans. This move to the rez could turn out all right after all.

I mingled with the crowd and got introduced to a lot of my relatives, from young kids to older adults. There were aunts, uncles, cousins, second cousins, great-aunts—you name it. Many of them looked vaguely familiar from my summer visits. But I knew I wouldn't remember most of their names.

The great thing was that everyone looked pretty much like me—I blended right in.

They all hung out for a couple of hours. Then, one-by-one, they drifted away. The only ones left were me, Nana, Pablo, and Adrian.

I sort of remembered Adrian from my summer visits here. He was introduced to me back then as an older cousin. It surprised me today to find out he was really my half-brother. My mom was his mom, but he had a different dad. He had a different last name than me because he took our mom's last name, Blackwolf. That's the name she had before marrying my father.

"Your mother was briefly with Adrian's father before she met your dad," Nana explained when we were alone in my room. "When your mother was pregnant with Adrian, the father left. He said he wasn't ready to be a dad. He never came back, and Adrian has never met the man."

"That's sad," I said as I unpacked my clothes.

"He stayed with me, and I raised him," Nana continued. "Your mother was young then. I wanted her to be able to go to college. That way she could get a good job and have a good life."

"That's where she met my dad, right?"

"That's right," Nana said.

"So he lives here with you?"

"Right down the hall from you," she confirmed. "You two will be able to get to know each other better."

I finished unpacking and putting my clothes away. Then I went down the hall to Adrian's room. I could hear Native American drumming and singing coming from inside. The door was closed so I knocked. In a few seconds, he opened the door.

"Come on in, bro," he said with a smile. He opened the door wide and returned to a workbench he had in one corner of the room. The drumming continued. It came from a speaker sitting on the workbench.

As I stepped into his room, I felt like I was stepping into another world. His walls were covered with posters and photos of powwow dancers, Native American clothing, beaded feathers, drums, and baskets. It looked like a museum.

I moved closer to Adrian's workbench and peeked at what he was doing.

"I'm repairing my choker," He said. "I've got to get everything ready for this weekend's powwow at Kumeyaay."

"What's a choker?" I asked. "Is it part of your Indian costume?"

He stopped what he was doing, turned down the volume on the music, and looked at me.

"I can't believe you just said that." He seemed annoyed. "When an American Indian person puts on his traditional clothing, that's not a costume. It's called 'regalia.' Or you can call it an 'outfit' when it's what a Native dancer wears."

"My bad," I said. "I didn't know."

"I don't ever want to hear the word 'costume' come out of your mouth again," he continued. "Unless you're talking about someone getting ready for Halloween."

Adrian turned the music back up and continued to work quietly. I just watched for a minute. Then I decided to try again.

"So what's a choker? Is it part of your regalia?"

"Better, dude," he said with a smile. "Yeah. It's worn tightly around your neck. That's why it's called a choker."

He held the choker up to his neck and showed me how it fit him. Then he went back to work.

I looked at the photos around the room some more. I saw that it was Adrian in his dance costume—oops, regalia—in some of the photos. He was dancing in some pictures and getting awards in others.

"Do you know anything about the powwow life?" he asked.

"No," I admitted. "It looks like hard work."

"I guess it is," he replied. "But once you catch the powwow bug, you get hooked on it. It's such a great way to connect with your own culture and be with other Native people."

"Is the powwow part of Chumash culture?" I asked.

"No, it's from the Plains Indian cultures," he said. "But many tribes with different cultural backgrounds hold powwows now as a way of bringing Native people together.

The Chumash powwow is always held in October."

"How did you get started with powwows?" I asked.

Instead of answering me, Adrian got up and walked to his closet. From inside, he carefully removed a long wooden box. He set the box on his bed and opened it.

Inside was a strange collection of things: a bird's wing, a bird's claw, a large single feather, and other objects.

"These belonged to our Crow grandfather," he said, pointing to himself and me.

Adrian picked up the wing and handed it to me. I looked at it closely, turning it over in my hands. The wing was actually a sort of fan. It had a handle that was covered with leather and beadwork.

"Grandpa told me the wing and the claw came from a golden eagle he found in Montana," Adrian said. "Our grandfather was a powwow dancer, and I'm following in his footsteps."

"I never knew anything about this," I said. This was like uncovering family secrets or something.

"The great thing about you and me is that we've got both Chumash and Crow blood," Adrian explained. "The Crow people are Plains Indians, and much of the powwow culture comes from those tribes."

"Isn't it kind of confusing to be from two tribes?"

"Not at all," Adrian said, turning to face me. "It's like having windows on two worlds. You can learn from them both. Take what you need from each. They're both part of you."

He paused and looked at me. "What was Mom like?" he asked.

"You didn't know her, did you?" I asked.

"No."

There was a little sadness in his voice. It reminded me of how much I missed her. I realized that it was better to have known her and lost her than not to have known her at all.

"She was really great," I replied cheerfully. "The best. You would've really liked her when you were my age."

"I'm glad to hear it," he said, still with sadness.

"After she died, Dad said she always knew what I was doing. She was watching from up there."

Adrian just listened.

"And I know she's been watching you, too."

He perked up a little.

"I bet she's seen every powwow you've ever danced in," I added.

"That's what Nana told me, but I thought she was just saying it," Adrian replied.

"I don't doubt it for one minute," I said, looking him straight in the eye.

He looked away, kind of letting our conversation soak in. Then I noticed a videocassette sitting in the bottom of the box. I picked it up and read its hand-written label: "Gathering of Nations, April 1996."

"You've got to see this," Adrian said, taking the video from me. He inserted it in an old VHS video machine in the corner of his room. He pressed play, and a grainy image appeared on his TV. The beat of a drum came through loud and clear.

The shaky camera panned across a large basketball court. The stadium seats were filled with Indians. The court was filled with powwow dancers. The camera zoomed in on one older man dancing. I recognized my grandfather from the pictures I'd seen of him.

"Grandpa was a good dancer," Adrian said. "And this is the year he won first place in the Men's Traditional Golden Age category at one of America's largest powwows."

"Wow!" I said.

"No. PowWOW!" Adrian said with a laugh.

"That's funny," I said.

Just then Nana's voice came ringing down the hallway.

"Dinner's ready! Come and get it!"

Adrian turned off the tape and the light on his workbench. We went to the dining room and sat down to an unusual dinner that Nana had cooked for us.

"Mark, these are foods from all of your cultural backgrounds," she explained. She pointed to different dishes as she named them. "This bowl of noodles is pansit from your Filipino relatives. The fry bread is what your Crow ancestors ate in the early reservation days, and what we still eat. The trout, which the Chumash have always eaten, comes from right here in the Santa Ynez River. And I know you're familiar with beans and tortillas from your Mexican ancestry. That's actually the food of the Indians there, before the Spaniards came."

"It all looks good," I said.

"*Comamos!*" Pablo said in Spanish.

"Let's eat," Nana translated.

And we did. I discovered that my ancestors really knew how to find and fix very good foods.

Chapter 4
My New Home

As the days went by, I had to get used to a different pace of life. Before I got here, I thought there wouldn't be much to do. But I was wrong. There was always something going on in a family this big. There were birthdays, baptisms, weddings, sporting events, Native American cultural events—always something.

It was great to learn that most of the people who lived on the reservation were mixed-bloods. They all came from at least two or three bloodlines, so I didn't feel so different.

"Our history is in our blood," Nana explained one afternoon. We were drinking lemonade under a big oak tree in her backyard. You could hear water running in the creek a few feet away.

"What do you mean?" I asked.

"Let's take you, for example," she said. "You're Chumash, Crow, Mexican, and Filipino, right?"

"That's what Mom and Dad always told me," I said. "Dad is Filipino and Mexican. Mom was Crow and Chumash."

"Did you ever wonder how those different kinds of people came together?"

"No, I guess I didn't," I answered. "Now that I think about it, I never really asked. I just accepted it."

"That's called the family tree. Each of us has one, with many roots and branches."

"Okay. I get it."

"The four different branches of your family tree have come together to make you. Each branch is worth knowing. And each one has a history, a story behind it."

"Adrian told me a little about my Crow branch," I said. "But I really don't know much about the Chumash branch either. I barely remember a few things Mom said."

"Chumash people have lived in this valley for at least ten thousand years," she said. "Our ancestors were smart people who learned to live in harmony with the land. Their village sites are scattered all over this area."

There was a kind of pride in her voice when she spoke about the Chumash.

"Then, in the 1700s, the Spaniards discovered the California region," she continued. "They moved in and took over. They built the missions, told us they'd teach us a better way of life, and caused us to lose our traditional ways." Her voice was sadder now.

"After that, we were overrun with waves of outsiders looking for land and wealth," she finished.

"Why couldn't they be stopped?" I asked.

"There were just too many of them," Nana answered. "They had better weapons, and horses, and they had a plan to take the land right out from under us. And they passed laws saying that we didn't have any rights. California Natives almost completely died out."

This wasn't any history I'd ever learned in school. It was all kind of depressing.

"But look at us now," Nana continued. "We're making a huge comeback. We've been able to start relearning our own culture and language, and even buying back land that was taken from us."

"What was it that changed?" I asked.

"A lot," she answered. "New laws were passed about tribes and tribal governments. More Natives got educated and learned to work within the American system. And most Americans learned to be more accepting of cultural differences."

"Okay. What else?"

"One big thing was money. Regular income. Something we never had before. For generations we were nothing more than servants and laborers in white peoples' homes."

She pointed toward the tribe's casino that sat a few hundred feet away.

"But things started to change in the 1980s. Congress passed laws that allowed Indian tribal governments to build casinos. That started right here with tribes in California."

She became lost in her own thoughts for a minute. Then she looked at me.

"But enough about that," she said. "Time to get your suitcase packed. You'll need enough clothes for a four-day trip."

"Where are we going?"

"We're going to take Adrian to his next powwow," Nana answered. "There's a powwow somewhere in California almost every weekend of the summer and fall, you know."

"Where is this powwow going to be held?"

"At a reservation near San Diego," Nana replied, with a twinkle in her eye.

"I thought you said you never go to San Diego," I protested.

"I was just kidding!" she said with a smile. "You'd better connect with your friends down there so we can make arrangements to pick up your surfboard. We're leaving tomorrow morning, a whole day early, just for that."

I was too excited for words. I immediately ran back to my room, fired up the laptop, and went online. I let the guys in San Diego know I'd be coming their way, and then I packed my bag for the trip.

The following morning, on Thursday, I was packed and ready to go. I stepped out the front door to find a huge RV parked in the street. A large tipi had been painted on the side, along with the words "Indian Country Traveler."

The RV's side door opened, and out stepped Adrian.

"Bring your bag on over so we can pack it away," he called to me.

"Where did this come from?" I asked.

"We keep it parked behind the neighbor's garage," he replied as he opened a storage door on one side of the RV. "They have more room over there."

I shoved my bag in alongside everyone else's luggage in the compartment. Adrian closed and locked the compartment door.

"Pablo does most of the driving," Adrian said as I followed him into the RV. "But I'm learning how to handle this monster on the highway."

Nana was already in the RV, sitting in the front passenger seat.

"We're just waiting for Pablo to finish checking the house and lock it up," Nana said.

Adrian and I sat down on the couch in the middle room of the RV. Soon Pablo stepped on board with a smile.

"*Vamonos!*" he said as he took the driver's seat.

"Let's go!" I successfully translated, and we pulled slowly away from the house.

I had never ridden in an RV before. The huge thing swayed back and forth a little on the highway. I'm glad I brought plenty of things to do on the five-hour drive.

We arrived at the RV campgrounds near San Diego at about three o'clock that afternoon. It was sunny and warm, a great day for the beach. My friends Chuck, Michael, and Daniel were waiting at the meeting place we'd arranged. I was so glad to see them, and my board!

We spent the rest of the day enjoying the surf, sand, and sun. My dream of getting back to the beach with my friends finally came true!

All too soon the sun set into an orange-colored ocean, and my friends went home. I don't know why, but as I watched my friends leaving, I felt as though the childhood part of my life was coming to a close. It wasn't a sad feeling, really. It just *was*.

Chapter 5
PowWOW!

We were all up early the next morning. I could tell Nana, Pablo and Adrian had been through this routine many times. Each had a job to do to get the RV packed, closed up, and ready for the road.

By nine o'clock we rolled into a nearby McDonald's and had breakfast in the parking lot. And by noon we arrived at the Kumeyaay reservation's RV campground. We were one of the early arrivals, so we got to pick a good place to park the RV.

All through the day and into the night, others arrived at the grounds. Cars, pickup trucks, vans, campers, RVs—you name it. Native people showed up in every kind of vehicle.

I tagged along behind Adrian as he meandered through the campsites visiting with friends he'd made over the years on the powwow trail. There were lots of them, and he introduced me to every one.

That afternoon I followed Adrian to the powwow arena so he could check in. As we went along he explained how things worked.

Each dancer who wanted to participate in the dance competition had to pay an entry fee, register for a dance category and age group, and then get a number. Their numbers were printed on a square of paper that had to be pinned to their dance regalia. That way the judges would give the correct score to the right dancer.

As I stood in line with Adrian waiting to register, more Indians of all ages came by to say hello to him. They came from tribal communities all over the state. I'd never seen so many different kinds of Indians in one place. For my brother, it was like a family reunion.

"Where did you meet all these Indians?" I asked him after he'd registered.

"At other powwows," he said. "I've been doing this for at least four years. That's one of the things I love about it. You make new friends from all over the place."

"The first Grand Entry will be at seven o'clock tonight," the lady at the registration table said. "We expect you to be lined up at the area's eastern entrance and ready to go by six forty-five."

"I'll be there with bells on," Adrian said with a laugh.

When we got back to the RV, Adrian pulled out several suitcases from the storage compartment. Each suitcase held some part of his dance regalia. It was fascinating to watch him take out all the pieces and put them on. He described each piece as he dressed.

On the upper part of his body he put a bone breastplate over a Native-style ribbon shirt. He wore a breechcloth that covered a pair of black gym shorts that no one would see. A fringed apron with front and back panels hung from his waist.

"I compete in the Men's Traditional dance category, young adult division," Adrian said as he slipped a pair of beaded moccasins on his feet. "Each dance style has its own type of regalia. You'll see when everyone lines up for the Grand Entry."

While Adrian and I had waited in line, Nana cooked dinner for us. Now Adrian took a break from getting dressed just long enough to sit down and eat.

All around us in the campground there were other families doing the same things we were. Some family members were putting on dance regalia. Others were cooking food or watching out for little children. The whole place was a beehive of activity. Everyone had a job to do or a place to be in order for the whole event to work.

After a quick meal, Adrian went back to dressing. The next step was war paint. While looking in a mirror, he applied blue paint to his forehead. Then red and white vertical stripes covered the rest of his face. When the blue paint had dried, he went back and painted a series of white stars above his eyebrows. Now his face looked like a patriotic American flag.

Then he slid on armbands and leg bands, followed by a pair of beaded cuffs that fit around his wrists. On his head he tied something he called a roach; it was made of long, stiff porcupine hairs that danced a little with each step.

He wasn't kidding about the bells, either. One of the last things he put on were two sets of round bells that had been sewn onto leather straps. He tied a leather strap to each ankle. When he took a step, the bells clanged.

Finally, he tied a large feather bustle to his lower back. This was made of long, beautiful feathers arranged in a circle around a centerpiece. It looked like rays of light shooting out from the sun.

When he was all dressed, Pablo pinned Adrian's competition tag—number two forty-five—to the front of his regalia. It seemed like almost every inch of my brother was covered, from head to foot and front to back.

The whole outfit reflected a red, white, and blue color theme. It was really spectacular.

Nana took a picture with her smartphone of me and Adrian standing together.

"What's the prize if you win your dance category?" I asked, looking at the photo on Nana's phone. I figured the winners would get a trophy or a blanket or something like that.

"Cash prizes are awarded to the top three places in each category," Nana answered. She picked up a poster from a nearby table that announced the Cahuilla powwow.

"Cahuilla's top prize for each category is one thousand dollars," she said, showing me the prize money printed on the poster.

I was speechless. A thousand dollars?

"Each host tribe offers different amounts," she continued. "Third place is usually two hundred fifty dollars."

"But if you aren't in the top three places, you get zero," Adrian added. "Just the feeling of knowing you're part of a shared intertribal culture."

"Wow," was all I could say.

Pablo was keeping track of the time so Adrian wouldn't be late for the Grand Entry lineup. At six thirty he said, "*Vamonos,*" and we all walked with Adrian toward the arena.

The Kumeyaay powwow arena had been set up on the tribe's baseball fields. There was a round center arena for the dancers. Around the edge of the arena were seats for the drummers and singers, with an additional row of seats for spectators. It looked like there were half a dozen drum groups set up.

Beyond the arena seating were the booths where vendors sold every kind of Native food, clothing, jewelry, and artwork you could ever imagine. People were busy looking over all the things for sale.

As we got close to the line of dancers, an announcer's voice boomed over loudspeakers placed around the arena.

"Calling all dancers," the announcer said. "Grand Entry in fifteen minutes. Line up at the eastern entrance of the dance arena. Our arena director will make sure you get lined up in the right order."

I was amazed at how many dancers were showing up for the line. Men, women, boys, and girls of all ages were finding their places in the growing line. Their dance outfits presented splashes of wild color, frantic feathers, beads, blankets, and shawls.

At the front of the line, a group of Native men and women in military uniforms were standing around chatting. Each held a flagpole or a long pole with feathers attached to it.

"American Indian veterans always bring in the flags and eagle staffs at the front of the line," Adrian said. "Honoring our warriors has always been part of the powwow tradition."

I just watched all of it come together. Seeing it for the first time had an impact on me I couldn't explain. It felt like something inside of me was moving around, shifting. It was an exciting feeling.

"Five minutes to Grand Entry," the announcer's voice bellowed from the loudspeakers. "Be there or be square," he added with a laugh.

"We'd better get to our seats," Nana advised. "Earlier this afternoon Pablo set up our folding chairs on the far side of the arena."

She looked Adrian over one last time to be sure that every part of his regalia was in place. Then she gave him two thumbs up.

"Thanks, Nana," he said as she was leaving. "Love you."

"Love you more," she said with a smile. I thought he would've been embarrassed by that coming from his grandmother, in front of all those people. But he wasn't. I looked around and saw other family members making sure their loved ones were in the line of dancers. Generations of Native people were involved with each dancer.

It was then that I realized that this powwow thing was more than just a hobby. More than just a way to pass the time. It meant something. It was very old, but still somehow very modern. I thought I might like to be a part of something like that.

Nana and I got to our seats just as the drum started pounding and the Grand Entry song began. The beat grew louder and the voices gained strength as the veterans and the dancers filed into the arena one at a time. Something within that drumbeat was pulling at me. It might sound corny, but I'd even say it was calling to me.

The line of people began to circle the outer edge of the dance arena, moving in a clockwise direction. All the spectators stood up to respect the American flag and the eagle staffs that led the way.

The line continued around the arena. When the front of the line had completed one full circle, the leaders carrying the flags moved inward, but kept circling. This formed the first layer of a spiral as more dancers came into the arena and the line continued.

What I was watching was hard to put into words. There was a lot to see and do my first night at my first powwow. All the sights, sounds, smells, and tastes flooded my brain. It was exhausting and exciting at the same time.

The first round of dance competitions ran on for several hours that night. I paid close attention to each of the dance categories to see how they were different from each other. But it was all starting to boggle my mind.

After a while I sat back in my chair and closed my eyes. I just listened to the sounds of the powwow as I sat with Nana and Pablo waiting for Adrian's round to be called.

Then finally the announcer said, "It's time for the young adult Men's Traditional competition. All dancers in this category make your way to the arena."

I perked up and focused back on the arena. Six dancers took up positions in the arena, including Adrian. Three judges stood nearby holding clipboards. The announcer gave the cue and the drum group started the song.

The dancers in this category looked like they might have been hunters out in the woods searching for deer. Or they could've been warriors on the plains stalking an enemy.

Their movements seemed to tell the story of some adventure they were experiencing. I thought Adrian was outstanding. He was like a time traveler from the past. He was showing me what life was like for my own ancestors.

I leaned closed to Nana and said, "I think I want to do this."

"Really?" Nana said. "Why?"

"I'm not sure. It's just so intense. It seems like it would make you forget about everything else that was happening in your life."

I watched Adrian until his dance competition ended. All the dancers but one took their last step with the last beat of the song. That dancer took one extra step, and I could tell he wasn't happy about it.

They all froze there for a few moments, holding a final pose. Then the spectators applauded loudly.

The announcer's voice boomed over the loudspeakers. "Heeeee yah! Lookin' good, dancers. It's like watching an episode of *Dancing with the Stars*!"

He laughed and the audience laughed with him. Everyone was having a good time.

I leaned over again to Nana and said, "Now I'm sure I need to do this. This is almost as good as surfing."

Chapter 6
The First Step

When Adrian finished his round of competition he came over to where we were sitting.

"Mark has something he wants to tell you," Nana said.

"What is it?" Adrian asked.

"I want to become a powwow dancer," I said. "I need you to show me how."

Adrian looked at me for a minute. He picked up a hand towel that Nana brought and wiped the sweat off his face. He looked at me again.

"You're not kidding, are you?" he said.

"No, I'm not," I replied.

"You show up at your first powwow, and all of a sudden you think you can dance," Adrian said in disbelief. "How is that even possible?"

"I don't know," I answered. "I—"

"Don't talk to me right now," Adrian said. He was almost angry, but I wasn't sure why. "I'm going to change out of my dance outfit."

He marched off toward our RV. I looked at Nana to see if she knew why Adrian was acting that way. She just shrugged. She, Pablo, and I gathered up our folding chairs and followed him.

By the time we got back to the RV, Adrian had calmed down. As he changed his clothes, he said he needed to explain a few things to me. Nana and Pablo went inside the RV so we could talk.

"Deciding you want to get involved in the powwow is a serious thing, man," Adrian said. "You can't just snap your fingers and, poof, you're a powwow dancer."

"I know that," I said.

"There are steps to follow," he said without looking at me. "Cultural protocols."

"What's a protocol?"

"It's the way things are done," he said. "It's the stuff you're expected to know in order to do something the right way."

"I'll do whatever it takes," I said.

"This is something that Nana and Pablo have to agree to, because it will require their time and energy. Not to mention the money involved."

He was getting worked up about this all over again.

"I get the picture," I said. "I'll talk it over with Nana."

"And another thing," he said. "You have to stick with it. You can't just decide one day to get involved, and then a few days later decide to drop out. It takes commitment."

"Okay, okay, okay," I finally said. "I get it. You don't think I'll take this seriously, and therefore you don't want me to do it. Is that it?"

Adrian took a deep breath before speaking.

"No, it's not that I don't want you to do it," he said. "I'm sorry if that's the way it sounded."

He had finished changing clothes, and he sat down to put on his shoes. After tying his laces, he paused and looked at me.

"All right," he said. "You have to answer one question before we go any further."

"Sure. Ask me."

"Why do you want to do this?"

I took a deep breath before answering. Then I told him the truth, even though it sounded kind of weird.

"The drum called to me," I said simply. "When the Grand Entry began, the drum started pulling at me. Like a magnet. I can't explain it any other way."

Adrian just looked at me for a long minute.

"What?" I asked, when he didn't say anything.

"That wasn't the answer I expected," he replied. "I thought you'd say it was because it looked neat. Or you wanted to impress your surfing buddies. Or some other shallow reason."

"Oh," I said. "Is that all? Well, I also have to admit that it does seem like a great way to meet girls."

We stared at each other for a second, and then Adrian broke out laughing. I let out a loud, deep laugh, too. And it took us a couple of minutes to recover.

"Okay, bro," he said when the laughing stopped. "You passed the first test. Welcome to the powwow trail."

That was the day I began my journey as a powwow dancer. Somebody once said that a journey of a thousand miles begins with one step. That was my first step.

When we got back home, Nana, Pablo, Adrian, and I sat down for a family meeting. Adrian laid out all the things I needed to do. In addition to picking a dance category and making a dance outfit, there was an important step I didn't know anything about.

Before I could dance at my first powwow, I'd have to host a "give-away." That's a time-honored tradition during which the family of the new dancer gives gifts to important people within the powwow circle. This happens during a break between the regular dance sessions at a powwow.

I would need to collect hundreds of things like blankets, towels, dishes, hats, belts, and other things that people in the powwow circuit could use. These things would then be given away to all the people who were involved in putting on the powwow. It was like a formal announcement that told the powwow world that you were serious about this.

Nana and Pablo had, of course, been through this process when Adrian started dancing. So they knew all about it, and readily agreed to organize it for me.

"This is all pretty overwhelming," I admitted during our family meeting. "I really didn't know fully what I was getting us all into, did I?"

"Good thing for you that we knew what you were getting us into," Adrian laughed.

All of them promised to support me any way they could. I, in turn, promised to make the commitment to see it through and do my best with all of it.

I had studied all the different powwow dance categories and decided to follow in Adrian's footsteps in the Men's Traditional category. He said that was the best option because Crow was one of the tribes that dance in the Traditional category. I'd be in the teen division.

"That's good," Nana said. "That'll speed things up. We kept all of Adrian's outfits that he outgrew, so we already have most of what we'll need to create your first set of regalia."

During the daytime, Adrian started teaching me about the Men's Traditional dance style. He said there were several different kinds of songs in this category, each with its own type of dance steps to go with it.

"There's the Crow Hop, the Sneak-up, and the Duck and Dive," he explained.

I laughed when I heard the names. I couldn't help it. They sounded so funny.

"Laugh all you want to," he said sternly. "But each one has a story behind it, a meaning, that is older than any of the music you hear on the radio today."

I could see he was serious, so I stopped laughing and listened.

"The important thing to remember about tribal dancing is to feel the music and the beat," he instructed. "Don't think about it too much. That'll just get in the way."

"Okay," I said.

"If you need to think about something while you're dancing, think about your Crow ancestors," he advised. "What was it like for them out on the hunt or in battle? What was it like living in a tipi and moving to follow the buffalo so everyone in the village could eat?"

At night, I worked with Nana to create my first dance outfit. She laid out regalia from two of Adrian's earlier outfits. I could see that parts of both outfits were worn out in places. She pulled out pieces from each of them that we could use to make a single nice outfit.

"One of the optional pieces of the Men's Traditional dance regalia is something called the coup stick," Nana said one night as she,

Adrian, and I worked. She said the letter *p* was silent in this word and pronounced it "koo."

"In the olden days, when the Crow lived on the open plains," Adrian said, "one of the things a warrior had to do to become a war chief was to hit or touch an enemy without killing him or being killed by him. That was called a coup. It showed that you were brave. The stick you used to touch the enemy with was called a coup stick."

Adrian took a long wooden box out of his closet and set it on the bed. Opening the box, he took out a long object wrapped in deer hide. Inside the hide was an old stick covered in beadwork. At the end of the stick was the claw of a bird with its talons ready to strike.

"This was our grandfather's coup stick," Adrian explained. "Nana gave it to me when I started dancing, but she wanted me to just keep it and not use it."

"That way it could be passed on to your kids and to their kids," Nana added.

I took the stick and turned it over in my hands. The beadwork was beautifully done.

"That's the claw of a golden eagle," Adrian said. "It came from Montana, where our Crow relatives still live."

I handed the coup stick back to him.

"So, if you want, you could have a coup stick of your own as part of your regalia," Nana said.

"Where can we get one?" I asked.

"Right here," Adrian answered.

He pulled another box out of his closet and presented it to me. Setting it on the bed, I opened it. Inside was another coup stick with a beaded shaft, leather strips hanging from one end, and an eagle claw on the other end.

"Awesome!" I shouted, turning the stick over and over.

"We ordered this from a Crow elder after you said you wanted to dance," Nana explained. "It just arrived in the mail."

I hugged them both and then pretended I was dancing in full regalia at my first powwow. The coup stick really gave me a feeling of power. I imagined what it must have been like to be a Crow warrior on the plains a hundred and fifty years ago.

I got goose bumps, along with a mental image that flashed through my mind. For one second I thought I was on a horse riding fast in a group of fellow warriors. In another second the image faded. Now I knew my dance outfit was complete.

Other things started falling into place too. When other members of the family heard I was going to start dancing, they began dropping by with gifts that I could use for the give-away.

In one short month, we had put together all the things I'd need to hit the powwow trail. Adrian said it took some people a year to get ready. It was mid-August and already almost time for school to start. So it was good that we'd gotten so much done so quickly.

Adrian showed me the list of upcoming powwows that he was planning to attend. He had to choose events close to us because of school. We'd couldn't head out until after school was over on a Friday, and we had to be back in time for school the following Monday.

So we planned to host my give-away at the Pala Tribe's powwow the weekend before school started. The Thursday night before the powwow, we stacked all the give-away stuff in the RV's back bedroom. It was piled floor to ceiling.

When we got to the powwow grounds the next day, Adrian made all the arrangements for the give-away with the arena director and the emcee. They said we could hold the give-away Saturday afternoon before the dinner break.

At around three o'clock that afternoon, several of Adrian's powwow friends came to the RV to help us unload the gifts. We started piling them up behind the emcee's table.

At four o'clock the emcee announced my give-away over the loudspeakers. He explained, "This afternoon we are welcoming a new dancer to the powwow world. His name is Mark Centeno from the Chumash

Reservation. He is of the Chumash and Crow Nations and is the younger brother of Adrian Blackwolf, well-known in powwow circles."

It took about an hour for the give-away. After all the gifts were given out, the main drum group started playing an honor song. My family and I began circling the arena. As we moved past the arena seats, dancers joined in behind us. Spectators also fell in the circle. Soon we were followed by a couple hundred people, all honoring the powwow tradition and welcoming me to their world.

When it was all over, Adrian said, "Now all these people are kind of part of your family. If you ever need anything, they'll do whatever they can to support you. In turn, you must be available to help out any one of them if they need it."

"That's kind of a big responsibility," I said.

"Powwows are based on things that Native Americans think are important," Adrian explained. "Honor, respect, tradition, and generosity."

"There's so much that goes into this," I observed. "It's a lot more than just dancing. Where did you learn all this stuff?"

"It started with Grandpa," Adrian replied. "He began teaching me when I was little. He grew up in a powwow family from Montana. The rest I learned from other people along the powwow trail. So will you."

That night, as I lay in bed trying to fall asleep, powwow songs rang in my ears. The faces of people who'd danced with me flashed in my mind. The beat of the drum pounded in my chest. It must have been midnight before they all faded away so I could get to sleep.

Chapter 7
The Powwow Trail

School started a few days after my give-away at the Pala powwow. I had to forget about the whole intertribal cultural thing for a while and turn my attention to the classroom.

The Santa Ynez Valley High School was located only a few blocks from the reservation. It was an easy walk back and forth each day. No waiting for a bus or a carpool.

I quickly discovered that several of my extended Chumash family members went to the same school. That was both a good thing and a bad thing. Good because I already knew a few kids at my new school. Bad because anything that happened at school was immediately known by everyone else in the family. And everyone on the rez. Bye-bye privacy.

Back in Texas, Dad did get himself a laptop so we could email and message each other. He began contacting me once a week. We set this up for Wednesday nights. I missed him, but this helped.

"I think it's rad that you're involved with powwows," Dad said online.

"Rad?" I shot back. "That's so twenty years ago, Dad. I don't think the teen slang works for you."

"Okay, sorry," Dad replied. "I think it's great that you're involved with powwows. It's character building and good exercise. But schoolwork has to be your number one priority."

"I know," I agreed. "Nana said I could do my weekend homework in the RV while we're driving to a powwow or coming back."

"That's fine, but I'm going to check in with Nana to make sure you're doing that," he replied.

We put the RV homework rule to the test the very next weekend. We headed out for the Serrano powwow Friday afternoon. This would be my first full competition.

The Serrano Reservation was located in the California desert, east of Los Angeles. When we got there, the camping area was already jam-packed with RVs, vans, and tents. But friends of Adrian's had reserved us a spot in the crowded campground.

Adrian and I got to the registration table just before they closed down for the night. There were still a few dancers waiting in line ahead of us. I introduced myself to the teen dancer at the end of the line. He was a little taller and heavier than me and looked a little older.

"I'm Mark, and this is my first competition," I said with enthusiasm. "Teen Men's Traditional."

"The name's Charley," he said. "Same category. You probably heard of me. Where are you from?"

"Chumash Rez, up near Santa Barbara," I answered. "Sorry, I haven't heard of you. Where are you from?"

"I live in LA, but I'm Lakota—Pine Ridge," he said. "My dad's a Native actor. He's been in several movies."

"Cool," I said.

A space at the registration table opened up, and the registrar said, "Next."

Charley was next in line, but before moving up to the table he said, "Sorry to say you'll be wasting your time and money this weekend. And every weekend for that matter. I never lose."

He turned and stepped up to the table to begin his registration.

I didn't know what to say, so I kept quiet. What Charley said about never losing might be true, but I didn't think he was supposed to be bragging to a beginner. Adrian had said that wasn't part of the spirit of the powwow.

When Charley finished registering, he turned to me.

"You know powwows aren't really meant for California Indians," he said. "You're all mostly watered-down mixed breeds. You should leave this stuff to real Indians like me."

Then he walked away.

What a rude put-down, I thought. I wasn't expecting this from another more experienced dancer. I didn't have a quick comeback for him. Adrian was standing behind me in line talking to one of his friends. But he heard what Charley said.

"Ignore him," Adrian advised. "I *have* heard of him. He's a well-known bragger. Powwow dance competition is more about doing your best than trying to beat everyone else."

I followed Adrian's advice and put Charley's put-down out of my mind. I had to prepare myself mentally for the next day's events. I registered and got my very first competition ID, number one hundred twenty-three.

The registration lady said there would be two Grand Entries on Saturday. The first one was at one o'clock in the afternoon. The second one would be at seven in the evening. Everyone had to dance in both to be eligible for the prize money.

I'll never forget what it felt like to dance in my first Grand Entry. I was part of a parade of dancing colors that moved in a slowly swirling spiral—like a kaleidoscope that you hold up to a light while twisting the outer ring. It was like everything that was good about being an Indian all rolled up into one totally awesome experience.

My first dance competition came late Saturday afternoon. When the emcee called for dancers in my category, Nana, Pablo, and Adrian all wished me good luck. Adrian stood at the edge of the arena with the video camera. He wanted to record my performance so we could talk about it later.

There were nine or ten teen Men's Traditional dancers who stepped into the arena. Charley, of course, was one of them. Three judges stood nearby, each with a clipboard to mark down scores.

I was nervous, but I tried to ignore it as the drumbeat began. I just started moving with the beat. As before, the drum pulled at me like a magnet. Its beat flowed through my body.

I had learned from Adrian that there was more than one style of song in the Traditional Men's dance category. A slightly different kind of dance went with each one. He said you had to learn the songs so you'd know which dance to do.

And there were parts of each song that had certain beats called honor beats. One of the drummers hit the drum very hard every other beat to create the honor beats. A dancer had to move differently during those beats to show that he honored the song.

Also, you needed to learn the songs so you'd know when the very last beat of the drum was coming. The most important thing was to stop exactly on the last beat and freeze in place. Otherwise the judges would give you really low scores or not even give you a score.

I was pretty sure this first song was a Crow Hop. During parts of this song, dancers were expected to move like a bird looking for food. You had to have a kind of hop in your step.

I felt awkward. My movements were unsteady. It was really the first time I'd tried to dance with all my regalia on. The extra weight made things even more difficult. I was beginning to feel self-conscious.

I saw the judges out of the corner of my eye. I could feel them judging me. I saw the other dancers moving so easily in time with the beat. I saw Charley across the arena showing off for the spectators closest to him. I had to admit that he looked very good. He moved like he owned the place.

Suddenly the song ended. I hadn't been paying attention and it caught me by surprise. I took an extra step after the final beat. I was immediately doomed to last place.

"Give our teen Traditional dancers a good round of applause, folks," the emcee said. "They've worked so hard."

The audience applauded for us. I looked over and saw Charley bowing to the people in the stands near him. These were clearly members of his fan club, if there's such a thing in the powwow circle.

I simply walked out of the arena toward Adrian, who had just finished videotaping the session. Adrian had told me that if you don't end properly, it's better not to waste the judges' time expecting to get a good score. It's better to just walk away.

"Let's give a hand to dancer number one-two-three, who is just leaving the arena," the announcer continued. "He's new to the powwow, but he knows enough to walk away out of respect to the other dancers. Better luck next time, young man."

The audience applauded respectfully.

"Go back out there and raise your coup stick with a smile," Adrian advised. "That shows you're a good sport."

I did as Adrian instructed, stepping back into the arena and raising my coup stick. The applause immediately increased. That made me smile. It made me feel that making a mistake was not such a big deal within the powwow family.

As Adrian and I walked back to our camp, he said, "I could tell that your mind wasn't focused on the song."

"You're right," I replied. "I was thinking about everything but the song."

"Don't sweat it," he offered. "It's easy to do—easy to get distracted by all the stuff going on around you."

"Did you see that kid Charley?" I asked. "He acts like a celebrity or something."

"The more you ignore him, the better off you'll be," Adrian advised. "Anyway, you now know what it's like to compete in the arena. Let's go celebrate your first competition."

"But I lost," I complained.

"No you didn't," Adrian explained. "You successfully gathered your regalia, learned the dance moves, had your give-away, and completed your first dance. That's a lot. I'm proud of you."

Put that way, it didn't sound half bad.

Chapter 8
The Son Who Returns

For the next couple of months I danced every weekend. It became easier and easier the more I did it. Nana, Pablo, Adrian, and I each had a job to do to make the traveling work.

We continued to mostly attend powwows fairly close by so we could make it to registration in time on Friday. Then when the powwows were over, we climbed back into the RV and headed home. I made sure I always did my homework so Dad wouldn't call the whole thing off.

As the weeks went by, I got better and better. I moved up from dead last to the middle of the pack. I was an average dancer and consistently came in about fifth or sixth in the competitions.

Charley was, of course, also at most of these competitions. And, of course, he always came in first, second, or third. Never any worse.

And he was, as ever, rude to the max, as Dad would say. One time I finished in fourth place, and I was feeling pretty good about it. It was the highest ranking I'd ever achieved. I was celebrating on the inside.

"Not bad for an apple," Charley said, coming up behind me after the competition ended.

"What did you say?" I asked. What he said didn't make sense.

"I said you didn't do bad for an apple," he said.

"What's that mean?" I asked.

"You've never been called an apple before?"

"No. Is it supposed to be an insult or something?" I asked.

"You're not as dumb as I thought," he replied. "Yeah, I'd say it's an insult. It means that you look like an Indian on the outside— with that red skin. But on the inside you're really not. You're white like the inside of an apple. Get it?"

He laughed and laughed as he walked away, back toward his own camp.

I just stood there looking at him. His so-called insult was mostly meaningless to me. I knew that Indians have always been thought of as being red. Red race, red man, red skin, and on like that.

I also knew I was two kinds of Indian and four kinds of brown. Not really anything white at all. So his words just seemed kind of pointless.

Back at our RV I told Adrian what Charley had said. Adrian just laughed.

"Charley's older brother said almost the same thing to me when I started dancing," he said. "At first, when Grandpa explained what it meant, I was mad. I wanted to hit the guy."

"What happened?" I asked.

"Grandpa also said Indians have been mistreated for so long by outsiders that it becomes a habit. When the outsiders aren't around to mistreat us, we Indians do it to each other."

"That sounds weird," I said.

"I know," Nana agreed as she came into the RV. "But your grandpa said that it was normal for people to do that kind of thing. When the white man moved into our lands and took over, they believed that Indians were less than human. The whites didn't allow us to have the same rights they had."

"I know a little about that," I said. "I learned some of it in a history class once."

"Right," Nana continued. "So when a person is made to feel inferior—that is, made to feel like they're not as good as other people—that person looks for someone else to put down. It's easy to believe that the only way you can feel okay about yourself is to act like you're better than someone else."

"That's really complicated," I replied. "You guys learned this from Grandpa?"

"Yes," Nana replied. "He said he wanted to understand what had really happened to our people in the past, so he took college classes in history and psychology."

"It's kind of over my head," I admitted. "but I'm glad you understand it."

"So my advice to you still stands," Adrian said. "Just ignore Charley. He's the one with the problem. He's the one who needs to get his mind right."

That was a lot to absorb at once. I thought about it all as we packed up the RV. It was the end of another powwow and time to head back home.

The first weekend in October is when the Chumash powwow is held each year. It takes place at the Live Oak Campground about fifteen miles out of Santa Ynez. We had loaded up the RV the night before, so when school let out on Friday afternoon, all we had to do was jump in the RV and go. Fifteen minutes later we arrived.

Huge oak trees covered the camping area and the powwow arena. It felt like we were miles and miles from anywhere. After we parked and set up camp, other cars, trucks, vans, and campers continued to pour into the grounds.

I was happy to see there was no sign of Charley anywhere. I felt myself relax knowing that I wouldn't have to confront him. I guess I hadn't realized that I was tense when he was around. I wondered if that had been affecting my dancing.

Anyway, the first Grand Entry wouldn't be until one o'clock on Saturday, so there was plenty of time for visiting powwow friends and all my Chumash family that came.

That night around a campfire, we shared memories and stories. My powwow family and my extended Chumash family merged together during that time. It felt very special. The only thing missing was my mom. She would've been right at home. I think she'd be proud of what I was doing.

Somehow Nana sensed what I was feeling. She moved closer to me and gave me a comforting squeeze on the arm.

"She's here you know," Nana said. "Her spirit knows what you're doing, what things you're going through. Don't ever doubt that."

I just nodded and hugged her. Sometimes it was hard to admit that I still needed my Nana.

The next day was even more special, if that was possible. The Chumash Powwow Committee had planned a special recognition ceremony for me. Since it was my first time to dance at the Chumash powwow, they called me up to the emcee's table right after the Grand Entry.

As I approached the front of the arena, the emcee announced, "The Chumash Elders Committee will make this presentation." The Powwow Committee members stepped back as the members of the Elders Committee stepped forward.

"We honor you because you represent the future of our tribe and because you are a descendant of our treasured ancestor Maria Solares," the head of the Elders Committee said. "She helped to preserve our language and culture so we could remember who we are."

Then a group of Chumash singers came forward to perform a traditional Chumash song in the tribal language. Their regalia was different than the style of regalia worn by other powwow dancers. It was simple and natural looking, made of deerskin decorated with shells, feathers, and parts of animal bones and antlers. The men wore full headdresses made of feathers that stuck out in all directions. The women wore hats made like small baskets turned upside down.

After that, Nana stepped out into the arena also dressed in Chumash regalia. I had never seen her wearing that outfit. She looked like some sort of Native royalty. She stood by me.

"My grandson, Mark, has come home to live with us on the Chumash Reservation," she announced to all the spectators and dancers. "Today I am giving him a Chumash name that he will be known by when he is here."

She looked down at me and smiled.

"From this day forth, you will be known as *Nik'oyi Wop*, the Son Who Returns."

The Chumash Elders Committee presented me with a Pendleton blanket and a Chumash basket filled with sage, pine nuts, acorns, and other Native things. They said these were all from plants used traditionally by the Chumash for food or medicine.

Everyone around the arena cheered and clapped for me. Shouts of *A-ho!* could be heard all around. Nana hugged me. The Elders Committee members shook my hand. It was all so unexpected. It was all so humbling. It all filled me with a strong sense of pride.

Chapter 9
The Lesson on the Bus

When the month of November began, the Chumash tribe held several events to mark that month as National American Indian Heritage Month. I hadn't heard of it before, but Adrian showed me a US government website that officially announced it.

"I saw where the Department of Defense made a big deal out of it for all the Indians who serve in the military," Adrian said. "They even let the Native soldiers hold powwows in Iraq and Afghanistan when they're off duty."

"I've heard that February is African American History Month," I told him. "So why doesn't anyone know that November is Indian month?"

"I guess because there are a lot more African Americans than Indians," Adrian said. "And they own more TV stations, radio stations, and newspapers than we do. They can advertise it and announce it all over the country so everyone knows about it."

"There should be a Native American TV channel," I suggested. "You could call it "Nativ" without the *e* at the end—NA-TV."

"You can build that with your first fifty million dollars," Adrian laughed. "I think that's about how much it would cost."

"Oh," I said.

"Enough about that," he said abruptly. "Time to focus on your last chance to dance and compete this year."

The final competition powwow of the year started on the Friday after Thanksgiving. I learned from Nana that it was also National American Indian Day. Another American Indian celebration no one ever heard of. Were we always this invisible, even when the country was supposed to be thinking about us?

"It became a national holiday just a few years ago," Nana had explained. "Congress passed a resolution and everything. No one has ever heard of it because most people in the country are usually spending time with their families on that day. If it was a school day, then you'd probably learn about it at school."

Thanksgiving night we packed up the RV. We left early the next morning. We got to the county fairgrounds where the powwow was to be held in the afternoon. That's when we found out we didn't have a place to park our RV. Adrian's friends who usually save us a spot couldn't come to this powwow.

So we had to park it a few miles away in a Walmart parking lot. Nana said that many Walmart stores around the country allow people to park their RVs in their parking lots when there is nowhere else to go.

Since we weren't camped right at the powwow grounds, it would be harder to get back and forth for Grand Entries and dance sessions. But Pablo had an idea. He had seen a bus stop at the street corner near the parking lot. He went over and looked at the bus route and schedule.

We were happy to learn that a bus stopped here at the Walmart every hour. That bus also went to the fairgrounds. So we were set.

Nana, Pablo, Adrian, and I must have been quite a sight to see as we waited at the bus stop. I had on my dance regalia. Adrian carried a small ice chest with our drinks and food. Pablo carried folding chairs, and Nana carried cushions and an umbrella to protect us from the sun.

People on the bus stared at us as we boarded. Some whispered to one another. But one little blond-haired boy about six years old came right over to me.

"Are you an Indian?" he asked. His mother ran over and tried to shush him and take him back to her seat.

"No, that's all right," I told her. "I'd like to talk to him." She backed off, leaving the boy with me.

"Yes, I'm an Indian," I said. "And so are my brother and my grandmother." I pointed to them.

"They don't look like Indians," he said. "But you do. You have on your Indian costume."

"What's your name?" I asked him.

"Roy," he said. "Roy Weatherby."

I reached out to shake his hand.

"My name's Mark Centeno," I said. "I'm pleased to meet you."

He put his hand in mine, and I gave it one firm shake.

"Roy, I want to tell you something," I started. "I *am* an Indian, and when an Indian wears his tribe's traditional clothes, it's not called a costume."

"What's it called then?" he asked.

"It's called regalia," I answered. "Can you say 'regalia?'"

"Re-gail-ya," he said very carefully.

I was kind of getting into this public conversation. It was a chance for me to show non-Indians what modern day Indians were really like, a chance to teach them something about who we are and what we do.

"Are you an Indian?" I asked Roy even though I already knew the answer.

"Well, of course not," he said.

"So if you put on Indian clothes, then it would be called a costume, because you aren't an Indian. Understand?"

"I think so. But why are you wearing your re-gail-ya? Is that what you wear every day?"

"I'm going to dance in a powwow. Have you ever been to a powwow?"

"No," Roy replied. He turned toward his mother and called, "Hey, Mom, can we go to the powwow to see Mark dance in his re-gail-ya?"

Everyone on the bus had been listening to the whole conversation, and now they all laughed. Roy blushed in embarrassment. His mother didn't answer her son's question.

"Roy, it's time to leave the nice young man alone and come back over here," she said.

"It's all right, Mrs. Weatherby," I said. "I'm enjoying this." I looked around the bus. "How about all of you? Are you enjoying this?" People nodded their heads and began clapping. That was pretty cool, I thought.

"You should let the boy go," a man said to Mrs. Weatherby. "He's obviously interested."

"We can't go now," Roy's mom said. "I have to get home and fix dinner for the family."

Just then the bus driver announced, "County fairgrounds, next stop."

Nana said, "We'd love to have you come and watch tomorrow, if you can. Mark will be in the Grand Entry at one o'clock, and he'll be competing at around three."

"Mom, please can we go?" Roy begged.

"We'll see, we'll see," his mother replied.

Nana, Pablo, Adrian, and I moved toward the exit.

"Hope to see you there, Roy," I called to him as I headed for the door. "It was nice meeting you."

Roy just waved and grinned from ear to ear as I stepped down off the bus. Everyone on the bus waved, too.

When we got to the powwow grounds, I registered for the competition as usual. Charley was there as usual. The tension in my body was also there as usual.

There weren't that many dancers competing in this powwow. When it came time for my category to compete, only five dancers stood in the arena. Before our song began, I looked over at Adrian to see if he was videotaping me again.

Then I had an idea. Why not videotape Charley so I could see what he did that always got him first, second, or third place?

I signaled to the emcee that I wasn't quite ready to begin. He nodded to me and indicated that he'd wait just one minute. I ran over to Adrian.

"Do me a favor," I whispered. "Videotape Charley this time. I want to study his moves later."

Adrian thought about it for a second and then nodded his agreement. As I turned to go back into the arena I spotted little Roy and his mother in the stands. I waved and gave him a big smile. He stood up and yelled, "Good luck, Mark!"

I realized I had my first fan. How about that, Mr. Charley Big-Shot Lakota Dancer! I ran back to my position and nodded to the emcee that I was ready.

"Take it away, Wild Horse Drum," the announcer said, and their song began. It started as a soft beat with a single drummer. Within a few beats it grew louder and stronger as all of the drummers came in. I started moving to the hard, steady beat.

It knew it wasn't a Crow Hop. It didn't have that kind of slower beat. It wasn't a Sneak-up either. The song didn't begin with a roll of the drum that sounded like gunfire on the battlefield. I realized it was a Duck and Dive song. Adrian told me this was an old warrior song from the Nez Perce or maybe our own tribe, depending on who was telling the story.

When the first set of honor beats came, all the dancers moved in a ducking motion, like they were dodging a cannonball on the battlefield. Grandpa had told Adrian that the idea for this song was based on an actual battle in 1877, when the Plains Indian people were being chased by the US Cavalry.

This time I only watched the drummers while I danced. I didn't look at Charley at all. I just felt the beat and relied on the practice I'd done. When the song ended, I stopped right on the last beat. I felt good about my performance.

The emcee gave the judges a few minutes to figure the scores, and then he called for an intertribal round dance. All the people in the stands came into the arena for a fun dance.

I walked over to where Roy and his mother were sitting.

"This dance is for everyone," I told Mrs. Weatherby. "You and Roy can come in and dance with me if you want to."

She said she was too shy to ever do anything like that, but it was all right for Roy. So I took Roy's little hand and we danced. I showed him how to move with the beat as we circled the arena. He was totally into it.

When the song was over I took him back to his mother.

"I'm glad you guys came," I told her. "You should take Roy whenever there's a powwow. You'd always be welcome."

She thanked me and said she'd try, but I didn't think she really meant it. I hoped she would for Roy's sake. I went looking for Adrian.

"Did you get it?" I asked when I found him. "Did you get Charley's moves?"

"Yeah, I got it," Adrian replied.

"Good. I want you to tape his other two rounds too. If we're lucky, we'll get a Sneak-up and a Crow Hop before the weekend's finished."

We had a Crow Hop that night and a Sneak-up Sunday afternoon. Adrian taped Charley both times. Look out, Mr. Charley Big-Shot Lakota Dancer. I'm going to be as good as you very soon.

Chapter 10
Winter Break

Winter in California is different from a lot of other places. I'd seen on the Weather Channel that it gets down below freezing for long periods of time in some parts of the country, and the snow blows and piles up several feet high for days at a time.

But here in Chumash territory, people think it's cold when it gets down to forty-five degrees. It's a really cold night when the temperature drops to thirty-two. It might get that cold only a few nights during the winter. That's why Californians are known as weather wimps.

But Nana said that no matter what the winter weather was like, many tribes spent the winters telling stories and tribal histories. It was a way of passing on traditions and tales to younger generations. A way of keeping those things alive.

So at the beginning of December, we had another family meeting to talk about what we were going to do during the coming winter. Nana, Pablo, Adrian, and I sat at the kitchen table drinking hot chocolate, even though it was a mild fifty-five degrees outside.

"Since you've been here, we've mostly focused on the powwow and your Crow side," Nana said. "But this winter I want to spend more time talking about your Chumash history and culture."

"Sounds good," I replied. "When I was honored at the Chumash powwow, and you gave me a Chumash name, I realized that I didn't know enough about my Chumash roots."

"We'll begin your Chumash lessons at the Winter Solstice," Nana said. "That's a very important time of year in Chumash culture."

"What's the Winter Solstice?" I asked. "I've never heard of that."

"It's the time of year, around December twenty-first, when the days are shortest," Nana said. "Special ceremonies are held to honor Grandfather Sun and to keep all things in the world in balance. But we'll talk about all this at Winter Solstice."

I had plenty to think about and work on until then. Final exams for the semester were coming up soon. Math and Spanish were my two worst subjects.

I'd decided to take Spanish so I could have conversations with Pablo. But conjugating verbs wasn't easy for me even in English. It was way over my head in Spanish. So I needed to get a little help outside of class on the subject.

One day, my Spanish teacher, Mr. Seleg, said I should come to his office after school to get the help I needed. So I knocked on his door on a Thursday afternoon in early December.

"Come in," he called from behind the closed door.

What a surprise I got when I stepped into his office. One wall was covered with surfing posters and pictures! An old longboard leaned against a corner of the room.

"You're a fan of surfing?" I asked, stepping closer to the wall of images.

"No, I'm a surfer," he said. "Been at it since I was about your age."

I looked closer at one of the photos. It was Mr. Seleg in a wet suit on a board, riding a five-foot wave!

"What about you?" he asked. "Ride the waves?"

"Are you kidding?" I said, turning back to him. "I grew up surfing down in San Diego. I sure miss it."

He motioned for me to take a seat in the chair in front of his desk. I sat.

"What are you doing during the winter break?"

"Hanging around here mostly," I said.

"Then you're officially invited to go surfing with me sometime over the holiday."

"Really? Awesome!"

"What board do you use?" Mr. Seleg asked.

"A Firewire Spitfire," I answered.

"That's a good short board, I hear. Easy to handle. My main board is a Stretch Fletcher Four-Fin."

"That one requires special skills," I said. "You must be good."

"I had my day," he said. "Won a few trophies." He looked over at his photo on the wall. He had a faraway look in his eyes.

"But we'd better get down to business," he said finally.

So we waded into my problems with Spanish. After a few tutoring sessions, I started catching on and began doing better in class. I think I did okay on the final exam.

On December twenty-first, we attended the Winter Solstice celebration held in the Chumash Elders Park. Before the ceremony began, Nana introduced me to an older Chumash man with long grayish hair.

"This is our *paha*," Nana said. "That's Chumash for ceremonial leader."

I shook the man's hand. He was wearing regalia like the Chumash singers had worn during my honoring ceremony at the powwow.

"You are the one called Nik'oyi Wop?" he asked.

"Yes, the Son Who Returns," I replied.

"I wish more of our young people still received their Indian name as they did in the old days," he said. "I am called *Kilik Ku,*" he said. "That means 'Hawk Person' in the Samala language."

"Samala? What's Samala?"

"That's our word for ourselves and the name of the language we speak," he answered. "Though we are Chumash, we are the Samala Chumash from this area right here. Other groups of Chumash in other areas have their own names for their groups as well."

During the ceremony, Kilik Ku brought out a huge quartz crystal that had been kept in darkness since June twenty-first when the Summer Solstice ceremony was held.

Nana explained that at the summer ceremony, the crystal absorbs the sun's rays. Those rays are then released into the atmosphere at the darkest time of the year. That signals the sun to start returning to its highest place in the sky.

After the ceremony, when we were having refreshments, Kilik Ku came over to me and Nana.

"I'll be leading winter sweats over at the sweat lodge behind the health clinic," he said. "I'd like to invite Mark to participate."

"That would be a good thing for you to do," Nana told me. "It fits right in with your Chumash cultural education."

"Okay, if you say so," I replied. "But I've never been in a sweat before."

"We'll go easy on you," Kilik Ku said.

Although Dad and I had been regularly instant messaging and talking on the phone, I still missed him. That's why I was really glad to see him when he flew to California to visit for a few days. He came to the reservation to see Nana and pick me up. We spent four great days together, including most of Christmas day. Then, late in the afternoon, he had to get back to Texas so he could go to work the next day.

My first sweat was the day after Christmas. I put my swimsuit on under my clothes and carried a towel with me as I walked to the lodge.

About a half dozen adults and youth gathered for the sweat, which was to begin about five o'clock in the evening. Kilik Ku promised that it wouldn't be too hot in this sweat since there were several people who were new to the experience.

Hawk Person explained to us that before we arrived he had selected the stones to be used and had prayed over them. He and his assistant had placed firewood in the fire pit, then arranged the stones on top of the wood.

Now the stones were getting red hot, so hot they glowed. Kilik Ku said everything in the ceremony was done in fours or groups of four. There would be four rounds in the lodge.

In each round he would sing four songs. Each of those songs contained four verses.

Hawk Person entered the lodge and took up his seat by the door, which was really a flap made of canvas. We took off our street clothes and entered the lodge one at a time, crawling on hands and knees. When everyone was seated inside, he signaled for his assistant to start bringing in the stones.

The whole process was very intense and not something I can really even explain. What happened in the lodge was something bigger than just the parts I could tell about. More than the darkness, heated rocks, steam, and songs that made up the ceremony. It wasn't exactly magic, but it was close to that. And I don't mean the cheap magic tricks you get in a kit. I mean it felt like I was connecting to the earth and the air and my own self for the first time.

When the last round was finished and Kilik Ku opened the flap, we crawled outside. I was very surprised to find that it had gotten dark. What I thought had taken about an hour had really lasted four hours.

As I dried myself off and drank some cool water, I looked up into the night sky. Spread out above me like millions of crystals were stars that were brighter than I'd ever seen them. I could clearly see the belt of stars that made up the Milky Way.

By the time I got home, I had a neck ache from looking up at those stars. I had also stepped in a hole and run into a couple of bushes, I was so focused on the sky. I collapsed into my bed, and when I opened my eyes a few moments later, it was morning. What a night!

My first surfing session with Mr. Seleg came the following Saturday. Nana had given me permission to go surfing with my Spanish teacher because he was already a family friend. Adrian had him for Spanish, and he'd been to Nana's house for Chumash events.

We met him in the high school parking lot that morning. He drove a cool 1970 VW van that had been repainted and fixed up. Real retro. He strapped my board next to his on the roof rack, and we zoomed away as fast as that forty-year-old, air-cooled engine could take us.

"Do you have to dodge stand-up paddle-boarders where you surf?" I asked as we drove along Highway 101 toward the ocean.

"No, we'll probably be the only ones on the water where we're going," he said with a big grin. "We're surfing an area along the Gaviota Coast, just off the Foxen Canyon Ranch. You have to own property there to even get access to the beach, which I do."

"Awesome," I said.

The Pacific Ocean was always freezing cold, no matter what time of year. I'd learned that from all my years of surfing in San Diego. I was glad I could still fit into my wet suit, but I'd grow out of it within a couple more months.

There was nothing better in the world than to have the sun in your face, a board under your feet, and a wave chasing you from behind. I didn't realize how much I'd missed it.

We got in a good four hours of wave-riding that day, and I was exhausted by the time we arrived back at Nana's house. Pablo was there to greet us, and he decided to test my Spanish teacher's speaking skills.

After about a ten-minute conversation, Pablo gave my Spanish teacher two thumbs up, and we knew he'd passed the test. I only understood about every fifth word they spoke, and Mr. Seleg promised Pablo he'd have me speaking conversational Spanish in no time.

As my surfing Spanish teacher left, he promised we'd ride the waves again very soon.

The end of the year was just a few days away. When I thought about what I'd done in the last few months, I almost couldn't believe it was all real. So much had been jammed into so little time. I hoped the coming year would be half as exciting!

Chapter 11
A New Year

On New Year's Day, our extended Chumash family gathered at our house. We watched the Rose Bowl parade on TV, ate a huge dinner, watched a football game, played a couple of video games, made up silly New Year's resolutions, and took a walk along the creek. It was an all-day thing.

Everyone started to head out around sunset. When they'd all gone, Adrian and I planted ourselves in his room. He cranked up a powwow CD and we listened.

In a little while, Nana came into the room carrying a large, rolled-up piece of paper.

"I'd like to show you both something I've been working on," she said. Adrian turned down the music, and we made room on the bed for Nana to unroll the paper.

"This is your Chumash family tree," she said.

On the paper was a hand-drawn chart filled with rows of names and lines connecting the names. On the top of the page was written a title: "Ten Generations of a Chumash Family."

"What's the earliest date you see on the chart?" she asked.

Adrian and I looked at the top of the chart. There was a woman's name in Spanish and the date of her birth.

"Seventeen forty-two," Adrian and I said at the same time.

"That's right," Nana confirmed. "A Chumash woman named Modesta was born about 1742. Modesta wouldn't have been her real name, her Chumash name."

"Why is that?" I asked.

"All the Indians who were taken into the missions were given Spanish names. They were also entered into the mission records, and I have traced those records generation by generation."

With her finger, she moved down the page, tracing a line of names, until she reached the bottom. There I saw my and Adrian's names.

"You and Adrian are the tenth generation of this family," Nana said. "Of course there are lots more generations that go back further, but these are the ones we have records for."

"Wow!" I said, a little in awe.

"We've lived on this land for at least nine thousand years according to anthropologists," Nana added. "Probably longer."

"Wow!" I said again.

Then Nana moved her finger back up to about the middle of the chart, stopping on the name Maria Solares.

"I remember that name," I blurted out. "You mentioned her at the powwow."

"Right," Nana agreed. "She was one of our most important ancestors."

Nana looked at Adrian.

"Tell Mark what you know about her," Nana told him.

"In the early 1900s, she worked with a guy named J. P. Harrington. He went around California taking notes about Native languages, stories, and traditions."

"Right again," Nana said. "He worked with Maria for three or four years, right here on this reservation, and wrote down everything she said. He took over one hundred thousand pages of notes about the Chumash."

"Wow!" I said a third time.

"That's why we honor her every year," Nana continued. "The missions had forced us to stop speaking our language and stop carrying on our traditions. But Maria had been taught all those things by her uncle when she was young."

"It's because of her that we've been able to relearn those things," Adrian added.

"Mixed in with everything else you'll be doing this year, we'll be studying the things Maria left for us," Nana said. "The stories she told and the words she spoke came from this place, right where we are. The more you know about your own ancestors, the more you'll know about who you are."

"Whoa," I said. "I never knew there was so much stuff to learn about being an Indian. I guess it's hard to know that you don't know what you don't know."

"What?" Adrian made a funny face.

"Did that make sense?" I said. Adrian thought for a minute.

"Yeah, in a weird way, it did," Adrian said.

"Well, I'm glad you got it," Nana said as she rolled up the family tree. "I'll leave you boys to your powwow music."

After she left, I told Adrian something that I hadn't said when we were making up silly New Year's resolutions.

"I do have a serious resolution," I said.

"Oh yeah, what is it?" he asked.

"My resolution is to dance at the Gathering of Nations Powwow in Albuquerque like Grandpa did," I said boldly.

"I like that resolution," Adrian replied. "That's a good one."

"But that's not all of the resolution," I added.

"Yeah? What's the rest?"

"I will beat Charley in the teen Men's Traditional competition at least once this year."

"What did I tell you about trying to beat other dancers?" Adrian reminded.

"I know what you said, but this is different," I answered defensively. "This is about Chumash pride. He claimed we weren't real Indians and had no place in the powwow circle."

"Yeah, I know he really goes too far," Adrian agreed.

"I don't want to beat him just to beat him," I continued. "I want him to know that being Indian is not about the color of your skin or how much is in your blood. It's about what's in your heart."

"Okay," Adrian said. "You know you really do surprise me sometimes."

"How do I do that?"

"Some things you say sound just like Grandpa," Adrian said. "Just like him. I think that old man speaks through you sometimes."

I just blinked. I could see he'd made his mind up about something. He turned the powwow music up and started to move with the beat. I stepped back to give him room.

"All right, Grandpa," he said to me. "Tomorrow we start working to make your resolution a reality. We will work night and day until we're sure you can beat Charley, to put him in his place and teach him that we are real Indians too."

With that, Adrian closed his eyes and concentrated on his movements. I could tell he was going deeply into himself. I had seen him do it before. He'd go deep inside and find someplace where extra power was stored. Then he'd come back to the surface with more energy than before. More determination.

I left him alone and went to my room. What an amazing New Year's Day it had been.

Chapter 12
The Final Push

My final push toward powwow glory began the very next day. Adrian pulled out all the videotapes he'd shot of me and Charley. Then he pulled out the videotape of Grandpa dancing at the Gathering of Nations. We would watch these together, and he'd give me his evaluations of what was good and what wasn't.

He put Grandpa's tape on, and we watched. The first shot showed the entire dance floor area, which was actually a basketball court. The hoops at either end of the court had been removed. That gave you a clear view of the entire arena.

What struck me immediately was how many dancers there were. It looked like more than twenty in each category. That made it kind of cramped, once you added the judges, who were standing nearby.

"That's more dancers than I've ever seen at one time," I said.

"It's always like that at the Gathering," Adrian replied.

The announcer gave the signal and the song began. The camera zoomed in on Grandpa and stayed on him. His movements were perfect. His steps were strong. I noticed that he proudly carried the coup stick Adrian had showed me.

There were two songs for each competition at the Gathering. Adrian said that was because there were so many dancers. The judges needed more time to be able to score each one.

Next we watched the tapes of me dancing. I was such an amateur that it was kind of embarrassing.

"Notice that with each competition, you get better and better," Adrian pointed out.

It was true. By the time we got to the last tape, I had become a lot better dancer. Then he put on the tape of Charley.

I could see right away that his moves were a lot like Grandpa's. I wondered why that was so.

"Grandpa was a Crow," Adrian explained. "Charley is a Lakota. Both are Northern Plains tribes that have been involved in powwow-style dancing for generations."

"Charley thinks we're only Chumash, which was not a tribe that originally practiced powwow-style dancing," I observed.

"So when you're dancing, you have to let your Crow side shine," Adrian advised. Then he moved closer to me and spoke softly.

"You have to call on Grandpa's spirit to help you," he said seriously. "Our ancestors are available to help us."

"All right," I said. "I'll call on Grandpa." And we spoke of that no more.

That afternoon my workouts and practice sessions began. I now had a better idea of what was needed to become a champion dancer.

I threw myself into it as if I were a boxer preparing for the next fight or a runner getting ready for my next Olympic challenge.

Adrian also had me lifting weights and sprinting around the high school track to build up my muscle strength. He said this would help me make power moves during honor beats and do the dives during Duck and Dive songs.

I had my first opportunity to try out my new skills early in March at the California Paiute Powwow. We pulled the RV into the campgrounds at about sunset that Friday. As I finished registering, who should show up in the line but Charley. Right on time.

"So you're back for more punishment, I see," he said. "I didn't think you'd last more than one powwow season."

"Sorry to disappoint," I replied. "I'm in it for the long haul. You see, my Grandpa was an all-star Crow dancer, from a long line of Crow dancers. And I have that blood in me."

I was surprised that he didn't have an immediate comeback. I walked away before he could think of some put-down. I think he was really surprised by what I said.

I came in third at that powwow. My highest place ever. I even won some cash, which I shared with Nana and Adrian.

Charley, of course, came in first place. But that didn't matter. I had done my best, and that was better than I'd ever done. So I was happy.

There were two more powwows before the Gathering, and I managed to place second or third in those. Charley had less and less to say as time went by. Even though I still hadn't beaten him, he felt me breathing down his neck.

The Gathering of Nations Powwow was usually held the last weekend of April. I wish there had been more powwows for me to compete in this season before that one. I needed the practice. But, as they say, it is what it is.

When it was time to head for Albuquerque, we didn't take the RV. We flew and then rented a car at the airport. And stayed in a hotel. It felt like first class all the way.

Our hotel wasn't too far from the University of New Mexico's basketball arena, where the powwow had been held for more than thirty years. The arena was called "the Pit" because the court was actually located lower than ground level.

From the street level you had to go down a steep set of steps to reach the floor. The court was surrounded on all sides by a steep set of seats, and those seats would be filled with people during every session of every dance competition. All the best dancers showed up for this one. It was like the Indianapolis 500 of the powwow world.

I got dressed at our hotel and was ready to head for the Pit when Nana stopped me at the door.

"Adrian and I have something to give you," she said. "We think it'll help you when you dance."

Adrian had kept one of his hands behind his back, and now he revealed what he'd been holding. It was Grandpa's coup stick.

"We want you to use this for all your competitions here in Albuquerque," Adrian said. "It will give you extra strength and bring you good luck."

I didn't know what to say. I took the stick from Adrian and turned it over and over in my hands.

"Wow!" was all that popped out of my mouth. My usual reaction to something spectacular.

"Remember Grandpa and how he danced," Nana advised. "No matter how you do in the competition, your dancing will be perfect."

I hugged Nana and Adrian real hard.

"Thanks, guys," I said, holding back a tear.

"*Apicho,*" Nana said. "That means 'good luck' in Samala."

"*Axay atiswin iwis pi'*," Adrian said with pride. "That means 'may spirit helpers be with you' in Samala."

"Pretty good, Adrian," I said with a smile. "Thanks."

"*Buena suerte,*" Pablo said in Spanish with great flourish.

"Good luck," I translated and laughed. "*Muchas gracias.*"

He gave me a hug too.

Just then a knock came at our hotel door.

"I have one more surprise for you," Nana said as she opened the door.

There stood my dad and Eleanor, with big smiles on their faces.

"Dad!" I screamed and ran to hug him.

"Hi, Eleanor," I said as Dad and I continued our hug.

"Hey there, Mark," she replied. "Good to see you. Your dad has been missing you."

"What a great surprise, on top of everything else," I said excitedly. "How long have you been planning this?"

"Nana called us in early January and told us about your resolution," Dad said. "That's when we decided to come. And Ellie made our airline and hotel arrangements the very next day."

"I'm glad both of you are here, Ellie," I said. "Thanks."

I shyly gave Ellie a hug.

Then we all headed for the Pit in the SUV that Dad had rented.

We arrived at the arena fifteen minutes later. What a mob. We waded through the thousands of people who'd come to see the dances and browse the vendor booths.

The Gathering of Nations Grand Entry was the largest I'd ever seen. And certainly the grandest. Hundreds of dancers slowly paraded into the arena, forming a huge, tight spiral. As the first set of singers finished their song, another drum group began a second song. And still the dancers moved around the floor until, at last, all of us were in the arena. It was overwhelming!

I'm glad I had watched Grandpa's dance tape, so it wasn't a shock to see two dozen dancers take the court when the announcer called for the teen Men's Traditional competition. And of course, Charley was among them.

It didn't matter. I felt confident in myself. I gestured toward him and said, "Good luck," loud enough for him to hear me. He gave me a little salute and surprisingly said, "Same to you."

I then scanned the crowd to find my family, and located them in about the middle of the seats near the dancers' entrance. I gave them a quick wave and smile, then turned my attention back to the floor.

I quickly closed my eyes and pictured Grandpa in my mind. "Be with me, Grandpa," I whispered and inhaled a deep breath.

Now everything was as it should be.

The announcer gave the signal and the singers began their first competition song. It was a Sneak-up, and I was glad. Grandpa had given his best performance here in the Pit during a Sneak-up.

As the drummers began the drumroll, I kneeled on the floor in about the same place Grandpa had all those years ago. I searched the floor and my surroundings as if I were looking for tracks and signs of an enemy. I became the warrior. Staying in a squatted position, I moved a few feet away and continued my search. I was completely focused and imitated Grandpa's movements as they played in my mind.

When the regular drumbeats began I stood up, thrust out my chest, and presented myself as a proud Crow warrior on the plains. The space I could move around in was limited because of nearby dancers, but I completely owned my ground.

When the song ended, I stopped exactly on the very last beat and froze in place. The huge audience erupted in the loudest applause I'd ever heard. I knew they were yelling and clapping for the whole field of dancers, but I felt proud to be among them.

I scanned quickly over to find my family and saw that they were all standing and applauding very enthusiastically. I smiled a proud smile and then returned my attention to the arena.

Some of the dancers stood in place as we waited for the judges to make their first round of calculations. Others moved around a little to keep their muscles loose. When the judges signaled the announcer they were ready, the second song began.

This time the singers gave us a Crow Hop. I was ready with Grandpa's coup stick, so when the honor beats came, I lifted it up to catch the spirit of the drum. It felt amazing! It seemed like the coup stick was actually capturing extra energy from the drum.

That boost of power brought more spring to my step, more strength to my legs. Suddenly I let out a war cry that I didn't even know I had in me. I surprised myself with it. At that moment it didn't matter who else was on the floor or how many people were in the arena. I was alone on the grassy plains, feeling my Indian identity, living in my Native pride.

My mind came back to the arena just as the song was coming to an end. I planted my foot firmly on the floor as the drummers hit their final beat. Boom!

Again the audience gave us a roaring round of applause. Again we dancers waited quietly for the judges to make their scores. When they signaled they were done, the announcer asked the audience to give us, and the drummers, one more round of applause.

I left the floor feeling very satisfied and complete. It was as if I had danced the perfect dance, the warrior's dance, and *that* was more important than winning.

My family and I celebrated being together with a big dinner at a nearby late-night restaurant. I told them that I didn't even care who won first, second, or third place this time, because my wish had come true.

I had attended one of the largest gatherings of Native people in the country. And I had danced the Men's Traditional style like my grandfather before me. I had achieved my personal best performance, and I had experienced what it might have felt like for my Native ancestors to live in their rightful place in the natural world.

Would I be among the first-, second-, or third-place winners at this powwow? I didn't know. Would I have beaten Charley when this powwow was over? I didn't care. All that mattered was that I had found my true identity in this life. And I had made strong connections to both of my tribal cultures. That was a lot to achieve.

And that was the source of my Native pride.

Chapter 13
Adrian's Last Words

I was happy to leave my story at the high point where I'd discovered who I was as a Native person. I no longer had anything to prove to myself or others.

But Adrian, ever the older and wiser brother, thought you'd want to know how things turned out at the Gathering of Nations.

I had two more competition rounds to complete during that last weekend in April.

Each time I danced, I ignored the people around me. I immersed myself in the music and the power of the song. Each time I felt my own heartbeat synchronize with the beat of the drum. It was as if the drum was beating from inside of me instead of it being something outside of me I heard with my ears.

Later, Adrian said he envied me. In all his years of powwow dancing, he'd never really experienced anything like that. Sure, he said, he'd come in first, second, or third plenty of times. But he'd never been transported out of this world like I had.

So when it was time to announce the winners, the announcer said, "In the teen Men's Traditional category, first place goes to Mark Centeno of the Crow and Chumash Nations."

Eleanor, Dad, Nana, Pablo, and Adrian were beyond excited. They clapped and cheered for me, but I was still in another world. What the announcer had said didn't sink in.

"What did he say?" I asked.

"You won first place!" Adrian shouted to be heard over the noise of the crowd.

"I did?" I was dumbfounded.

"Go up and get your prize," Adrian said.

I still didn't seem to grasp what was happening. Adrian walked with me to the front of the arena to help me pick up my prize.

The emcee also announced who had won second and third place in my category. Adrian said Charley's name wasn't mentioned. I didn't even notice.

But I did begin to realize that I'd achieved more than I'd ever hoped for. Gradually, I allowed the feeling of that success to sink in.

"This has been quite a trip," I said finally as we left the arena together. "Thanks to you guys. All of you."

As we crossed the parking lot and headed toward the SUV, we heard a voice from behind us.

"Mark, wait up a minute," a young man's voice called.

We turned to see Charley standing with a Native man who somehow looked familiar. I realized that it was Charley's actor father. I'd seen him in a couple of movies in past years.

Charley and his dad approached.

"Charley has something to say to you," his father said to me.

I looked at Charley and waited.

"Go on," his father said.

"I . . .," Charley muttered. "I'm sorry for the things I said to you," he finally blurted out. "I was being conceited and boastful, which is not in keeping with the traditions of my people or those of us within the powwow family."

He reached out his hand. I reached out mine. We shook.

"What else?" his father prompted.

"You're a real Indian too," he admitted, still holding on to my hand. "I'm half white and half Indian. So I'm not any more of a real Indian than you are. I'm sorry for saying that."

He dropped his hand from mine and looked down at the ground. Everyone was silent for a moment.

"That's all right," I said after a pause. "We all make mistakes."

Charley brightened and looked up.

"You were awesome tonight," he told me with excitement. "It was like you barely touched the ground. What was that?"

"I stopped thinking," I said. "I allowed myself only to feel. In my mind I saw my Crow grandfather as he had danced, and his steps became my steps."

Later, Adrian said they all just stared at me. This was deep stuff for a fifteen-year-old, he said.

"The more I know about my ancestors, the more I know about myself," I said. "Isn't that right, Nana?"

"Absolutely!" she agreed.

Charley's dad introduced himself and Charley to all of us in that parking lot. Afterward, Charley's dad invited us to the Frontier Restaurant and treated us all to a late-night dinner.

Charley and I sat together and talked

almost nonstop. You'd have thought we were old friends. Who knows? Maybe Grandpa had competed against Charley's grandpa all those years ago on a night like this at another Gathering of Nations powwow.

About the Author

Gary Robinson, a writer and filmmaker of Cherokee and Choctaw Indian descent, has spent more than twenty-five years working with American Indian communities to tell the historical and contemporary stories of Native people in all forms of media. His television work has aired on PBS, Turner Broadcasting, Ovation Network, and others. His nonfiction books, *From Warriors to Soldiers* and *The Language of Victory,* reveal little-known aspects of American Indian service in the US military from the Revolutionary War to modern times. He has also written three other teen novels, *Thunder on the Plains, Tribal Journey,* and *Little Brother of War,* and two children's books that share aspects of Native American culture through popular holiday themes: *Native American Night Before Christmas* and *Native American Twelve Days of Christmas.* He lives in rural central California.

7th GENERATION

PathFinders novels offer exciting contemporary and historical stories featuring Native teens and written by Native authors.

For information, visit:
NativeVoicesBooks.com

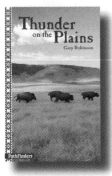

Thunder on the Plains
Gary Robinson
- 978-1-939053-00-8
- $9.95
- 128 pages

Tribal Journey
Gary Robinson
978-1-939053-01-5 •
$9.95 •
120 pages •

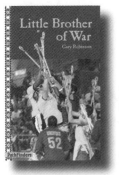

Little Brother of War
Gary Robinson
- 978-1-939053-02-2
- $9.95
- 120 pages

Available from your local bookstore or you can buy them directly from:

Book Publishing Company • P.O. Box 99 • Summertown, TN 38483
1-888-260-8458

Please include $3.95 per book for shipping and handling.